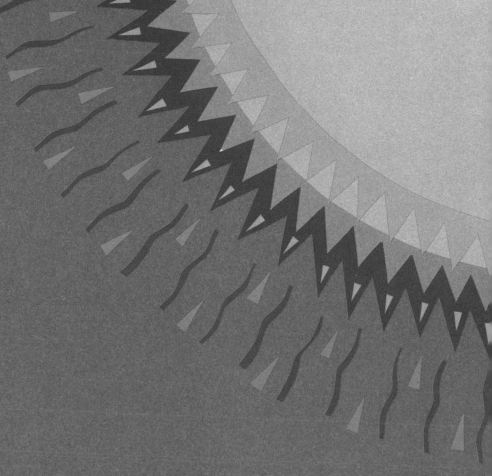

HOW GIRAFFE GOT SUCH A LONG NECK... AND WHY RHINO IS SO GRUMPY

A Tale From East Africa

To Mrs. Williams, Chloe, Sam, and Baby Jack
J. C.

About the Story and Art

Versions of this story are told in many parts of East Africa.
Similar tales are told by the Kikuyu and Masai tribes in
Kenya and by tribes in Southern Africa. This version has
been adapted by permission of Nick Greaves from an East
African folktale that appears in *When Hippo Was Hairy*
(David Bateman Ltd, New Zealand, 1988). The artist has
based his depiction of Man on early Masai tribesmen.

First published in the United States 1993 by
Dial Books for Young Readers
A Division of Penguin Books USA Inc.
375 Hudson Street
New York, New York 10014

Published in Great Britain
by Studio Editions Ltd as *The First Giraffe*
Text copyright © 1993 by Michael Rosen
Pictures copyright © 1993 by John Clementson
All rights reserved
Printed in Singapore
First Edition
10 9 8 7 6 5 4 3 2 1

ISBN 0-8037-1621-4
LC: 92-46662
CIP data available upon request

They walked and walked for a night.
Finally, just before dawn they saw
Man's hut in the distance.

The sun was blazing again when they
reached the hut.
"Man! We're starving. We're dying," said Giraffe.
"There's nothing for us to eat, nothing but dust."
"I know," said Man.
"Nothing except the juicy green leaves on the trees,"
said Giraffe, "but they're too high for us to reach."
"I know," said Man.

"Can you help us?" asked Giraffe.
"Come back tomorrow," said Man.
"I need time to prepare the magic herb."
"Will it help us reach the leaves on
 the trees?" asked Giraffe.
"Tomorrow," said Man.
"Tomorrow," said Giraffe.
"Oomph!" snorted Rhino.

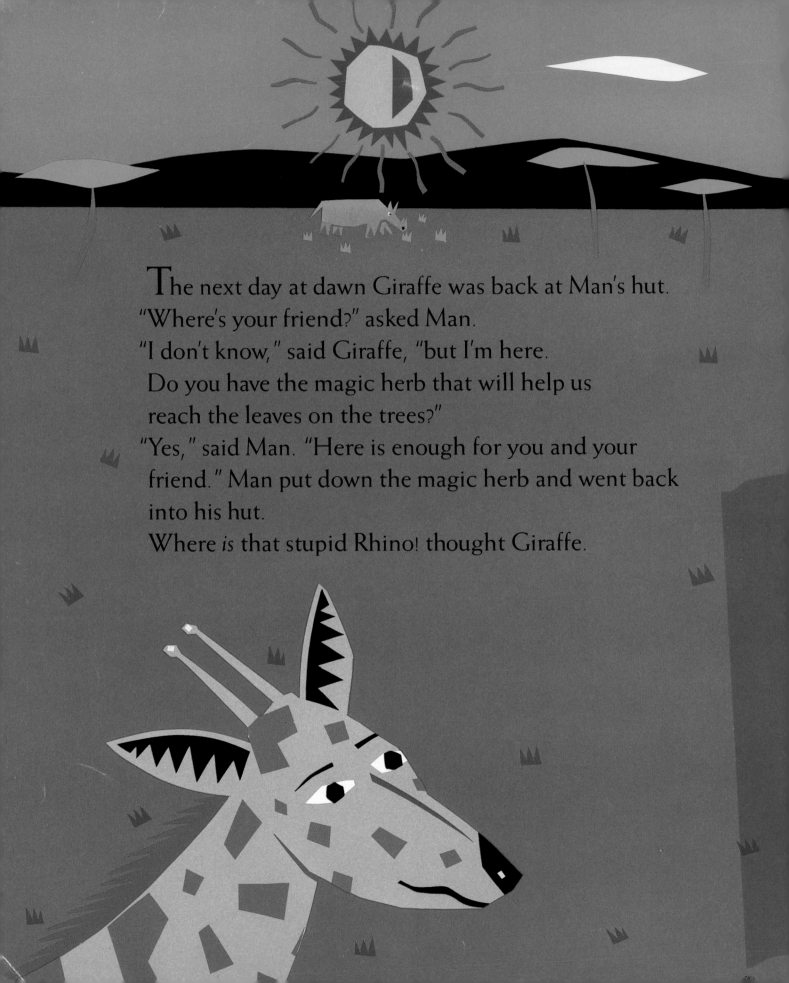

The next day at dawn Giraffe was back at Man's hut.
"Where's your friend?" asked Man.
"I don't know," said Giraffe, "but I'm here.
Do you have the magic herb that will help us
reach the leaves on the trees?"
"Yes," said Man. "Here is enough for you and your
friend." Man put down the magic herb and went back
into his hut.
Where *is* that stupid Rhino! thought Giraffe.

And so it is today that on the great African plains you can see Giraffe, the tall one, and Rhino, the grumpy one. Rhino is *still* cross with Man for giving away the magic herb, *still* cross with Giraffe for eating all of it, and *especially* cross with himself for not remembering to be on time for the magic.

"OOMPH!"